Sleeping Beauty

Sleeping Beauty

RETOLD BY *Adèle Geras*

ILLUSTRATED BY *Christian Birmingham*

ORCHARD BOOKS • NEW YORK
AN IMPRINT OF SCHOLASTIC INC.

This, too, is for Phoebe
–A.G.

To Isabella Francesca
–C.B.

Introduction

The story of Sleeping Beauty is a very old one. There are versions of it in many languages, but perhaps the best loved of all is the one written in the seventeenth century by Charles Perrault. It's called *La belle au bois dormant*, which means "the beauty of the sleeping wood." There is also a famous ballet called *The Sleeping Beauty* with music by Tchaikovsky.

One of the things I like best about writing new words for a well-known story is the chance it gives me to work a little magic of my own on a tale that never fails to please those who hear it. As well as powerful enchantment of every kind, a beautiful heroine, and a handsome hero, it has that element most important in any tale: a truly frightening villain in the shape of the malevolent fairy to whom I've given the name Skura, which seems to me pleasantly dark and sinister.

The best thing about the tale is this: We know when we start reading that there will be a happy ending — happily ever after.

— Adèle Geras

Once upon a time, there lived a King and a Queen who would have been the happiest people in their kingdom if not for the fact that they had no children. They lived in a palace surrounded by water: Flower beds, and box-hedges, and rose arbors covered the grounds on either side of the river. The silver water of the river flowed past beehives, through vineyards, and in and out of meadows and cornfields to the sea, which lay to the west. To the east, the forest stretched as far as the blue mountains.

The King and Queen had consulted every doctor and wise woman in the land. They dreamed each night of a child of their own, who would fill the palace with joy, but still the door of the palace nursery remained closed, for there was no royal baby for the Queen and her husband to care for.

One day, made weary by despair, the Queen sat on the riverbank and spoke to her own reflection in the water.

"If only we had a baby," she said, "I would do nothing but gaze at the cradle and rejoice in my good fortune."

Dragonflies flashed suddenly around her head, the leaves on every tree whispered to her, and she could hear a humming in the air which seemed to be saying, *Go back to the palace, and when the roses are in bloom, your baby will be born.*

The Queen, however, was filled with doubts. "How foolish I am!" she said, and she stood up and began to walk back to the palace garden. "The voices I hear are nothing but my desires and dreams speaking. I will put them out of my mind."

That evening, the King looked carefully at his wife.

"What is troubling you, my dear?" he asked. "You are quite silent tonight."

The Queen wondered whether she should mention the river and the humming voice in her head. She decided not to, and instead she said, "I was walking by the river today for a long time, and I am now very tired. I think I will go to bed after our dinner."

"I will wish you a pleasant sleep, dearest," said the King, "and the sweetest of dreams."

Nine months later, just as the roses were coming into their glory, the Queen gave birth to a girl. The child was named Aurora, and the King and Queen were filled with such joy that they decided she should have the most magnificent christening party anyone had ever seen. Therefore, they gave orders that the palace should be cleaned for the occasion, from the top of the highest turret to the bottom of the deepest dungeon.

Then pastry chefs began gathering ingredients for the cake: spices from the East, golden sugar from the New World, raisins dried from the palace grapevines, and nuts from every nut tree in the kingdom. Hunters brought deer to fill the venison pies; fishermen heaped their baskets high with fish and took them to the palace kitchens. Peacocks were stuffed, roasted, and decorated with their own tail feathers. The court musicians tuned their instruments and practiced every dance melody they knew. Gardeners carried a thousand roses into the palace, where the ladies-in-waiting made them into garlands whose fragrance lingered in every chamber.

"It will be a most splendid party," said the Queen. "And to mark the occasion, our darling Aurora will have the protection of wise women from every part of the kingdom. There are some who call them fairies, and it is said that these wise women have knowledge of all kinds of enchantment. I will send messengers to find them and invite them all to our feast, and I will ask the fairies to be guardians to our daughter."

A few days later, the messengers returned to the palace with seven letters of acceptance. From river, ocean, and desert, from the icy plains and the tropical jungles, from mountain and woodland, every fairy let it be known how delighted she would be to attend such a grand celebration.

"What luck!" cried the Queen. "Seven wise women have accepted, and we have exactly seven gold plates and seven matching sets of knives and forks and spoons."

"And there are seven crystal goblets, too," the King added, "which is extremely fortunate."

The King and Queen had forgotten someone, however. In a high tower built in a clearing in the dark and distant heart of the forest, there was one window in which a dim light was burning. This was where the very oldest fairy in the kingdom lived. Her name was Skura. She had retreated to the tower years ago and lived quite alone but for her gray cat and the other familiars who visited her from time to time.

"I am insulted," she said to the cat. "My bats and black-winged ravens have brought me news of a christening at the palace. Everyone but me has been invited to this feast. All the other fairies will be there and will eat and drink and dance by the light of candles. But I shall go uninvited, you may be sure." Then she smiled, and stroked the cat, who stretched and yowled and blinked his yellow eyes.

"I shall go," Skura whispered. "And I shall ride in the black carriage, I think. They will see what a terrible thing it is they have done by forgetting me."

The day of the feast arrived. A table had been laid for the feast in the banquet hall. The candles were lit, and their flames were reflected in every piece of gold, and caught in the dazzle of the crystal goblets.

But far away, in the dark heart of the forest, Skura had been readying herself for her journey. Just after sunset, she crept carefully down the steps of her tower and hurried into her carriage. It made its way along the forest paths, rattling like old bones, and as it drew close to the palace, storm clouds amassed above the turrets, and a sheet of lightning rippled across the sky.

Skura swept into the hall with her black cloak streaming behind her. The gray wolves who were her familiars padded silently by her side. She saw that the King and Queen were sitting on two thrones at the farthest end of the room, with the seven other fairies of the kingdom gathered around them. The newborn Princess Aurora was asleep in a cradle decorated with pink roses and tinkling silver bells, and everyone was gazing lovingly at her where she lay dreaming.

When the King and Queen caught sight of the latecomer, it

took them a moment to recognize Skura, whom no one had seen for years.

"Oh, dear!" cried the Queen with a shiver of dread. "It's you! How dreadfully careless of us to forget you! Please accept our sincere apologies and forgive us for our discourtesy."

She signaled to the servants to lay a place for the latest guest.

"You thought I was dead, perhaps," said Skura. "It is true that I have not been traveling in a very long time. If I may have a golden plate and a golden knife and fork and drink a toast to the new Princess from a crystal goblet, then we'll say no more about it."

"There are only seven sets of golden cutlery, and only seven gold plates, and see, even the Queen and I are not drinking from crystal goblets," said the King.

Skura looked at the chair which the servants were hastily pushing into place at the long dining table. Her mouth tightened into a thin line and she frowned.

"Ah, well," she said. "It cannot be helped, but this insult will have consequences, I'm sorry to say." The words were harshly spoken, and Skura's body was stiff with rage.

The Queen turned pale and twisted her hands together in her lap. "Let us continue with our celebration, friends. This is a happy occasion."

The fairy of the mist-wreathed mountains moved closer to the cradle. "We were just about to give the Princess our gifts. I say that she will be as beautiful as a wild, climbing rose."

"And I," said the fairy of the roaring rivers, "say that her voice will be as lovely as a singing stream."

"She will have the grace of a swan," added the fairy of the blue oceans.

"She will be strong," said the fairy of the icy plains of the North.

"And intelligent," said the fairy of the shifting sands of the desert.

"And kind," said the fairy of the tropical jungles of the South. She bowed gracefully to her companions and they returned her gesture with warm smiles.

Skura pushed her way into the circle around the cradle, and began to speak. Her words chilled the hearts of the King and Queen, as though a killing frost had fallen on the whole company.

"What I shall give little Aurora will perhaps not be quite what you would wish for," she said in a voice like a blade being drawn across stone. "All your gifts will be of little use to her, alas, for my offering" — she paused — "is a life cut short." The Queen swooned, and the King put his arm around her to steady her. "She may enjoy her grace and beauty and intelligence for sixteen years," Skura continued, "but then she will prick her finger on a spindle and fall down dead."

She turned and snapped her fingers, and the wolves, who had melted into the shadows in the corners of the room, came to her side, and she walked out of the room without looking back. Silence followed the words she had spoken — a hush so complete that every shadow seemed to thicken. The candles guttered. A howling wind beat against the glass of the high windows. The whole company of fairies stood as still as carved statues, and only after many minutes

was the silence broken by the cries of the Queen, who was weeping tears of anguish. Then the fairy from the woodland stepped forward. She spoke in a low voice, but every word fell on the air like a blessing, and the King and Queen felt the dread — which was like a sword of ice stabbed into their hearts — melt a little.

"Alas, I cannot undo every particle of magic cast by an older fairy, but I can say this: Your child will not die, Your Majesties. On her sixteenth birthday, she will prick her finger with a spindle, but then she will fall not into Death, but into a sleep which will last for one hundred years."

"One hundred years!" the Queen cried out in anguish. "We shall all be dead in one hundred years. What will become of our daughter without her mother and father?"

"She will wake from her enchantment," said the fairy of the woodland, "and it will be her destiny to be happy, I promise you that."

The King and Queen bowed their heads in gratitude, and smiled at the fairy.

"We thank you, kind friend, for your help," said the King.

"And we thank all of you for coming to this christening feast, which has been made darker than we would have wished. Now we must bid you good night, and wish you safe journeys as you make your separate ways home."

One by one, the fairies bowed and left the hall. They stepped out into the night, and the moon shone down on them as they went.

In the palace, the King gave the Queen his hand, and together they left the banquet hall. Two servants picked up the sleeping Aurora and followed them to the palace nursery. The King and Queen were too unhappy to close their eyes that night. They paced up and down, tormented by the thought of the future that the fairies had decreed for their precious child.

"No one," said the King, "may escape the fate that is in store for him, but nevertheless, I will not stand by and wait for this hideous prophecy to be fulfilled. Anything I can do — and there is much I can do, believe me — I will do to protect our Aurora."

Next morning, he summoned the whole court and made a proclamation.

"This," he said, "is my command. Every single spindle in the kingdom is to be destroyed. Everyone who brings a spindle to the courtyard in front of the palace during the next week will see it burned, and I shall give them five gold coins as a reward. After that, my soldiers will ride through the land seeking out those people who live in dwellings far from the palace and may not have heard my pronouncement."

The years went by, and the seasons turned. The leaves of summer fell from the trees, and winter lay over the land. The spindles had been burned in a huge bonfire, but long after the ashes were cold, memories of the christening remained, and everyone was filled with foreboding.

rincess Aurora grew up surrounded by love and care. By the time she was twelve, she was already a fine horsewoman. Accompanied by her attendants, she rode her favorite white mare through the fields and woodlands beyond the palace grounds, taking note of every bird that sang to her from the trees, and every creature that ran into the undergrowth as she passed by. She learned to shoot arrows from a bow, and the King's archery master told everyone he spoke to that she had as good an eye as any boy he'd ever taught. Falcons obeyed her when she whistled them down from the skies, and the royal ducks and geese came to eat from her hand when she walked beside the river. Her own pet dog followed her everywhere and spent each night curled up with her on a bedspread thickly embroidered with a pattern of silk roses stitched in pink and silver threads.

Aurora was as beautiful and graceful as the fairies had foretold, and she was as accomplished, too. The King employed the very best teachers to instruct her, and she read all the books that lined the walls of the palace library, marveling at the illuminated letters and delighting in every story and adventure. She loved the globe that stood in the schoolroom, and she gazed at it for hours, turning it gently and wondering about the lands she could see painted all over it. Her dancing master said she understood the measures of the music as well as he did, and her singing teacher pronounced her voice both pure and sweet.

Her mother instructed her in needlework. The two of them sat together beside the open window in the morning, sewing stitches into a cloth stretched over an embroidery frame. Pictures of mythical animals and fantastical birds and flowers grew under Aurora's fingers as she stitched.

"I would rather ride," Aurora said one day when the weather was warm and the sun shone in through the window, making diamond shapes on the floor of the chamber. "Embroidery is for winter nights."

"I know that you would rather climb a tree than sit beneath one," said the Queen with a smile, "and you may go out soon, my dear. Just finish that flower in the border. It will take only a few more stitches. And you may tell me what you learned in your lesson yesterday."

Time passed. Aurora's sixteenth birthday was approaching. As soon as the first buds appeared on the rosebushes, everyone in the palace began preparing the celebration. The King and Queen remembered Skura's wicked pronouncement, and also the words of the fairy from the woodland, and they trembled at the thought that their beloved daughter might soon be lost to them.

"We must hope for the best," the King told his wife. "I did my utmost to see that every spindle in the kingdom was burned in the bonfire."

"I know you did, my dear," said the Queen. "But still, I cannot help worrying."

The King said nothing, for he was worried, too, though he tried not to show it in front of his subjects. He took out the list of all the guests who had been invited to the ball in Aurora's honor and read the names out to his wife, hoping to turn her mind away from sadness.

urora's birthday dawned at last, and by nightfall the palace was filled with people who had come from every corner of the kingdom. The princess stood at the window and watched as all the guests arrived for the celebration in a fleet of riverboats, which the King had put at their disposal. They walked into the garden, where lanterns were hung from every tree. An orchestra hidden among the shrubs played music, and the smell of roasting meats filled the air. The King and Queen greeted their guests, and their radiant daughter — who stood beside them in a silken gown embroidered with tiny flowers and trimmed with white lace — was as beautiful as a rose and smiled at all who came to wish her well.

Aurora danced with every nobleman in the kingdom. Her silver slippers caught the light of the lanterns and glittered in the dusk. All the gifts that her guests had brought her were laid on a long trestle table. There were necklaces and brooches, and mirrors in silver frames engraved with silver flowers. There were books bound in white leather full of stories of love and adventure. There were silk

robes and golden shoes, and a chess set carved from ebony and ivory.

The night came slowly, and the sky turned from mauve to darkest blue. One by one, the guests went down to the river where the boats were moored, and the boatmen stood ready to take them home. The King and Queen were busy saying good-bye to everyone, and the Princess stood beside them. When everyone had gone at last, Aurora said, "May I walk for a while before I go to bed? It has been such a wonderful party, and I thank you both for it, but now I would like to be alone so that I may remember everyone's kind words and good wishes."

"Certainly, my darling," said the King, pleased that the occasion had gone so well.

Aurora wandered away from the garden. There was a smoke-gray cat sitting near the bridge, and Aurora made her way toward it.

"Who are you, cat?" she asked. "I have never seen you on the palace grounds before. What a beautiful creature you are! And what shining yellow eyes you have!"

The cat's eyes narrowed to half-moons of amber light, and it padded away. Over the bridge and to the foot of a deserted guardhouse tower, Aurora followed where the creature led. Looking up, she thought, *There's a light burning in that window up there. It must be someone's room. How strange that I have never noticed it before. I wonder, who can be living up there?*

When she reached the tower, Aurora did not hesitate, for she was as curious as any other young woman might be. She followed the smoke-gray cat and began to climb the stone steps. She was not at all afraid. What could there be to fear in a building so close to her own father's palace? True, the darkness was thick here, and a chill hung in the air, but the dark and the cold did not frighten her. She went up and up, following the spiraling staircase until she came to a heavy wooden door, which stood a little ajar. The Princess knocked on it and then knocked again, and before she could lift her hand a third time the door creaked and gaped a little wider, though no hand had opened it. She looked into the room and saw what appeared to be a serving-woman standing in front of her.

At first Aurora was surprised to see this old woman, but she had been brought up to be polite to her elders. "I'm sorry to disturb you, Madam," she said, "but there was a light burning in your window, and I was curious to see who could possibly be living up here."

"Come in, come in, my dear," said the serving-woman. "I have been expecting you."

"I was following a cat. A beautiful, smoke-gray cat," said Aurora. "But I can't see it anywhere now. Perhaps it's hiding." She began to look around.

The woman went to sit at a spinning wheel beside the hearth. She turned her face away, but the Princess noticed that her eyes were very much like those of the gray cat, and she wondered at the resemblance. For a few moments there was silence but for the turning of the wheel and the quiet hum of the wool as it was spun into fine thread, like a spider's silk.

"What are you doing, Madam?" said Aurora, who was interested in everyone and everything. "What is that you are holding in your hand?"

"This, my dear, is a spindle," said the woman. "Have you never seen one before? I am spinning wool into fine thread, which will then be woven into cloth."

"How wonderful," said the Princess. "I wish that I could learn to do it. Would you teach me, please?"

"Nothing in the world would give me greater pleasure," said the woman, showing grayish teeth in a false smile. "Come and sit down here, on this stool." She beckoned with her finger and smiled at the Princess, and Aurora went to sit down.

"You must hold the spindle like this," said the woman, moving it a little in the girl's hand.

"Oh, yes, I see now," said Aurora, but no sooner were the words out of her mouth than the spindle seemed to twist and twist again, and as quick as the blink of an eye the sharp point pricked the tip of her second finger. She had no time to cry out or complain. In the moment that it took for a drop of blood to fall from her finger and onto her skirt, Princess Aurora fainted away.

Skura looked at the body lying in the wide windowsill and smiled. "My work is done," she said to herself. "It has happened just as I said it would."

She left the room like a shadow, and made her way down the stairs. At the bottom, it was a smoke-gray cat with yellow eyes that slipped quietly out of the guardhouse tower. The creature found the path and followed it until it reached the deepest and darkest heart of the forest. In the distance, thunder rolled and birds with black wings flew up from the trees.

Before long, the King and Queen noticed that Aurora was still missing.

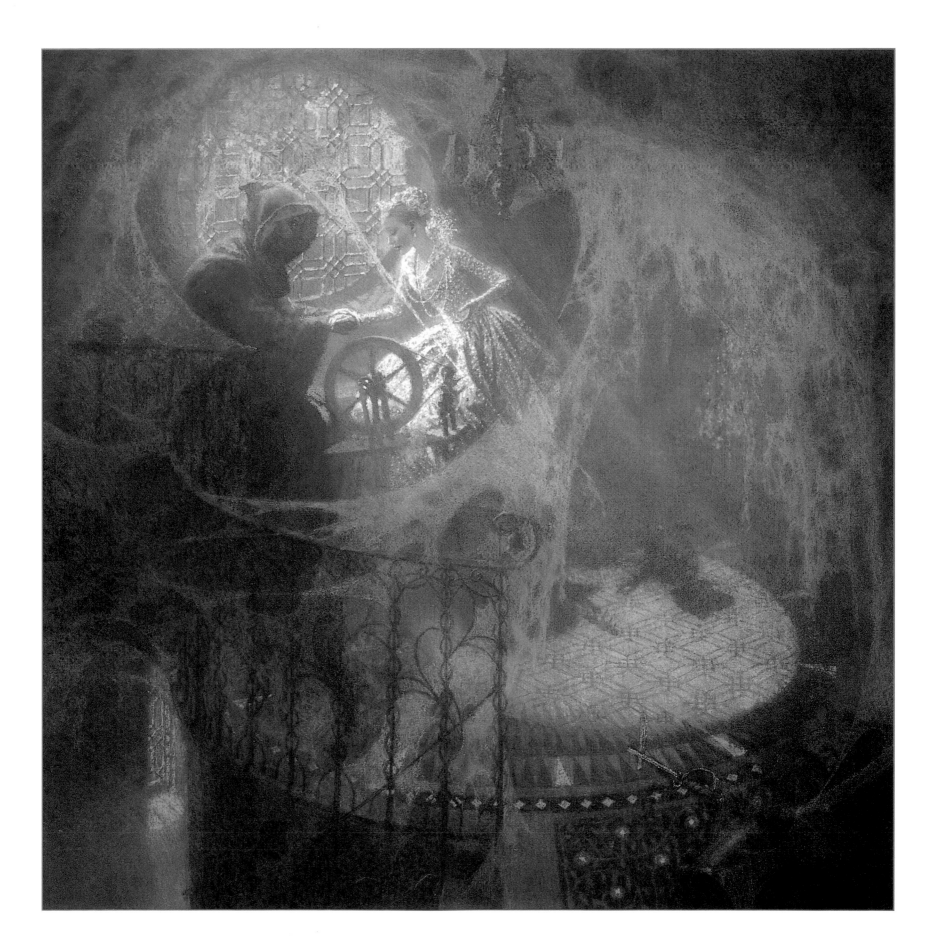

"We will search every inch of the palace and the grounds," said the King. "Do not worry, my dear, before there is need to. Surely we will find her safe and well. Perhaps she has gone to the stables. She loves to watch the horses being groomed."

The Queen said nothing, but her heart was weighed down with fear. Had she not been dreading this day for the whole of her daughter's life?

Servants were sent to look in every corner of the palace. They went everywhere, from the most distant part of the garden to the stables and the kitchens, and still Aurora could not be found. The King and Queen could not bear to sit idly and wait, and just before dawn they went into the courtyard to join in the search.

"We should not have let her out of our sight," said the Queen, "on today of all days. Have you forgotten the fairies' prophecies?"

"You know I have not," said the King. He noticed a black bird sitting on the railing of the bridge, and the sight of it made him shiver. As the King and Queen looked at it, the bird spread its wings and flew up and up to the highest window in the guardhouse tower, where it perched on a ledge.

"The guardhouse tower . . ." said the King. "No one will have thought to climb up there." Together they ran to the foot of the tower. The King flung open the door and hurried up the steps to the small chamber at the very top. The Queen ran after him, trembling with fear. As they crossed the threshold, they gasped in horror at what they saw.

"Aurora!" the King cried.

"Oh, my daughter! How did you come to be in such a place?"

The Queen could hardly speak for weeping. "Beloved child!" she sobbed. "Why did we not protect you? Why did we not prevent this from happening?"

Aurora was still breathing, and with a blush of pink still in her cheeks. The black bird sat unmoving on the window ledge, gazing in at the scene with its strange yellow eyes.

"Hurry!" said the Queen. "We cannot leave her in this dreadful place. Send for someone to carry her to her own room. She must be made comfortable."

The royal party left the tower, and four attendants carried Aurora to her own bedchamber. There, the finest silk sheets were already on the bed, and the softest pillows were in place. Aurora's dog was at the door, waiting for his mistress. A lady-in-waiting undressed the Princess, folded her clothes and laid them in a sandalwood chest. She took out a nightgown made from the finest linen and embroidered with golden birds and silver leaves, and she dressed Aurora in it. Then she laid her mistress on her own bed with

a coverlet of white wool spread over her to keep her warm through her long sleep.

The door of the bedroom opened and a servant announced the arrival of the fairy of the woodland, who bowed low as she crossed the threshold. She walked to the Queen's side and took her hand to console her.

"You must be brave," she told the Queen. "You must say farewell to your child, for you will not see her for a very long time. It would be too cruel to make you live in the world without her, and so you, as well as everyone in the palace, will sleep together with Aurora."

The King and Queen kissed their daughter and left the chamber. The Princess's dog jumped onto the bed and curled up at his mistress's feet. The fairy of the woodland raised her hands and spread magic into the air. A blue mist floated from the wall hangings to the painted ceiling. It slid under the door and down the staircase, and everything in the palace fell silent as it passed. The cooks in the kitchen yawned, and sat down, and put their heads on the table. The boy who was turning the spit fell asleep where he stood, and the fire that had been roasting a side of lamb dimmed to a glow and then went out. Footmen closed their eyes and leaned against the walls. Gardeners, cellarmen, beekeepers, archers, ladies-in-waiting, scullery maids, coachmen, and stable boys — every single person in the palace was as still and unmoving as a stone. Horses, peacocks, swans, ducks, geese, doves, bees, hunting dogs, and cats in the barnyard and kitchen, every one of them fell into a deep, deep sleep. The fairy of the woodland was pleased with her work.

As she crossed the bridge, she moved her hands once more, and the shrubs, flowers, and trees in the garden began to grow. "Now," the fairy said to herself, "everything may safely be left to itself."

ithin a few days, the walls of the palace were covered with ivy. Thick mats of water lilies almost choked the river so that it became no more than a thin stream. Roses grew tall and wild and formed a tight network of green, thorn-studded stems that climbed right up over the sills and crisscrossed the windows. Shrubs spread shoots over the ground so that every path disappeared, and beyond the bridge the trees of the woodland put out new branches which knotted themselves together to form dark thickets and tangled undergrowth. Crows made their nests in the trees, and thin gray wolves moved through the shadows of the forest.

Within a few months, the palace had vanished almost entirely. Only the tallest turrets were still visible when the weather was fine and there were no clouds to hide them. Years passed, and then more years, and everyone who lived in the countryside around where the palace once stood told tales about what had happened. These tales grew as wild as weeds. Some said that witches used the hidden palace as a place to celebrate their strange ceremonies. Others told of an ogre who waited for those unlucky children who managed to find their way through the woods. And there were those who believed that anyone who managed to reach the palace would find only ghosts drifting through every room.

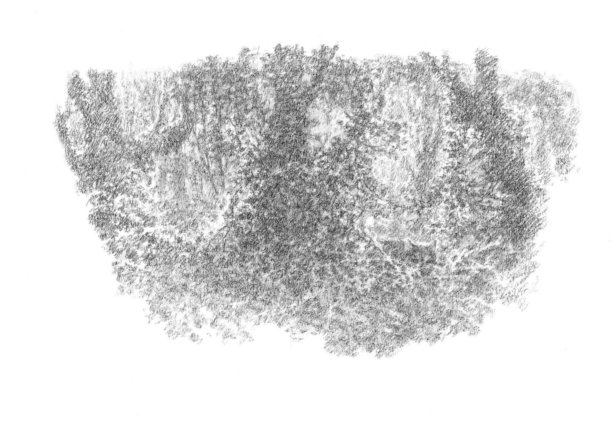

One year turned into another year, and then another. Stories were told in the kingdom about the hidden palace in the depths of the forest, and the more they were told, the less they were believed. After one hundred years had passed, only children and dreamers still wondered what had become of the sleeping Princess, whom no one would ever find because she was so well hidden behind high walls of thorny woodland and knotted rose stems.

One day, Prince Florian was riding through the forest with his friends. They had been hunting all day, and it was almost time for him to return to his castle that stood on the highest peak of a nearby mountain. Florian had heard tales of the enchanted palace, but how could he know that it was one hundred years to the very day since Aurora had fallen into her long slumber? The fairy of the woodland had been waiting for this moment, and when she saw Florian and his hunting party riding into a clearing, she made herself visible to them in the form of an old lady, carrying a bundle of sticks with which to light a fire.

"Good afternoon, Madam," Florian called out when he saw her, for he was both well mannered and cheerful. "Do you live hereabouts? Perhaps you can tell us if the stories we hear about this forest are true."

"We must make for our castle, Your Highness," said Florian's squire. "It is late, and you must not be absent from the evening feast."

"There will be time enough for that," said Florian, and

continued to address the old lady. "I apologize for my squire, but I am curious. Are the stories I have heard true?"

"That depends on what you've been told," said the fairy of the woodland.

"They say that there's a palace in the heart of this wood, guarded by monstrous creatures that would eat you with one snap of their jaws if you dared to enter."

"That is partly true," said the fairy. "There *is* a palace hidden in this forest, but it is not guarded, and, what is more, a treasure greater than any in the whole world is waiting for the person who is brave enough to venture into its darkness."

"I'm brave enough!" cried Florian. "Is it gold? Or jewels and silver? Tell me what I will find when I reach the palace, old woman."

"You will find your heart's desire," said the fairy. "There is no greater treasure in the whole world."

"Whatever the treasure may be," said Florian, "I feel it is my fate to find it."

"You will recognize it when you see it," said the fairy. "You must not look behind you, but continue making your way to the deepest part of the forest, and when you reach the palace, you will know what to do. Your heart will guide you."

"Thank you, Madam," said Florian. "I am most grateful to you. Here, take my cloak to keep you warm on your way home."

The fairy of the woodland smiled at Florian. "You are very kind, sir," she said, and she gathered the folds of the garment carefully around her. "Your kindness will be rewarded, never fear. Do not lose courage."

"You may be sure I will not," said Florian. He dismounted his horse and tied the black stallion to a nearby tree.

"Wait here, " he whispered to the animal. "I will return to fetch you when I've found my heart's desire."

The horse whinnied gently and rubbed its nose against its master's gloved hand.

The Prince's friends were worried. "You cannot go into the depths of such a forest all by yourself," said one.

"At least let your squire come with you," said another.

"Perhaps we can return tomorrow and make our way to the heart of the wood in daylight," said a third. "Twilight will soon be here, and the darkness. It's time to return to the castle."

"All of you must indeed return," said Florian. "I do not want anyone at all to go with me. I want to be alone to find my heart's desire. It is my destiny, I am sure of it."

"If you believe the words of an ancient crone," said another friend, "instead of the advice of your closest companions, then you are indeed a fool."

"And you are discourteous," said Florian. He looked around to see whether the old lady had heard these unkind words, but she had disappeared.

The Prince's friends turned their horses in the direction of the castle. "We will tell your father you have stopped on your way home to visit a friend," said one. "We do not wish to worry him with the truth. Good luck to you!"

Before Florian had time to reply, they were gone. His squire stood close beside the Prince's horse and refused to leave.

"I will wait here, my Lord," he said, and Florian smiled.

"I'm grateful to you," he said, patting his horse's side. "And I will doubtless be happy to see you when I come out of the wood. But I must go into it alone."

"Take every care, Sire," said the squire. "Darkness is nearly here."

It was true. Owls were calling from high branches. Thin, gray wolves with burning eyes slipped between the black trees, and the forest in front of him seemed impenetrable. It was a mass of twisted roots and undergrowth as thick as a wall.

Florian drew his sword and stepped up to a thick hedge of briars and vines tightly enmeshed. With his entire strength behind it, he brought the bright blade of his weapon down and hacked at the first branches. Again and again he struck, and it seemed to him that progress was going to be impossible, because as soon as one knot of wood was cut, there was another in its place. But he went on and on, hacking and striking, making, it seemed to him, no progress at all. Creatures fled into the undergrowth with a rustle and a hiss; birds flew up from their nests, disturbed by the noise, and rose up into the night sky. The wind began to howl through the trees.

Florian cut and cut as the gale raged around him, and thorns and twigs tore at his hands. When it was almost dark, after hours of toil, the branches began to yield a little, and then fell open of their own accord, as though two invisible hands had pulled them apart.

Florian stopped to rest for a while.

"Something very strange indeed is happening here," he said to himself. "Trees do not spring open without some human help. This must truly be an enchanted forest."

For a moment he hesitated, thinking that the old woman must have deceived him. He peered into the thicket and saw nothing but darkess. An owl swooped down from a hidden branch and passed him in a blur of gray feathers, and its cry made Florian shiver. But then he gripped his sword and felt new courage coming into his heart.

"I have to go on," he said. "I must find my heart's desire. I can deal with any dangers that I meet."

He stepped into the small gap where the trees had parted. As he continued to advance, it seemed to him that the undergrowth shrank away from his feet, turning black and disappearing as though an unseen fire were burning it away. To his right and left, the trees bent and swayed and leaned so far from the path that Florian found he could walk without any trouble.

I am like a sailor finding my way in a sea of trees, he thought, and the sound of the wind in the branches was like a thousand sighs. He looked behind him and saw that the path remained clear. The moon was high in the sky. Florian could not see the place where he'd left his squire, but the silver light comforted him. Turning, he concentrated on the path ahead of him.

I must be nearly at the palace, he thought. *I will not lose heart now.*

Step by careful step, he walked through a mile of trees and bushes, until at last he came to a bridge. Below him, the place where a river had once run was clogged with plants. Creepers had climbed up over the stone parapet and made a thick green carpet for Florian to walk on.

This bridge leads to the palace, he thought. Something was glittering in the moonlight. *Could it be a window?*

He peered into the breaking dawn. Ahead of him he saw a staircase leading up to a door. Everything else was quite overgrown with leaves and thickened stems and the faded flowers of one hundred summers, which had bloomed and died where they grew and now hung on every branch like ghostly lanterns.

Florian climbed up to the door and reached out his hand to pull at the plants that covered it. As soon as he touched them, they too curled up and died, and a wind sprang up and blew away what remained of them, like so much ash. Black birds, which had been nesting in the eaves, flew up and away, their wing beats breaking the silence.

He pushed the door open and stood in the great hall of a palace. Everywhere he looked, there were statues in the shape of human beings.

"These cannot be real people," Florian said to himself, "for real people would have died and turned to bones long ago, and these look exactly as though they are asleep."

He walked past a footman covered in the dust of years. He climbed up the main staircase, drawn on by a strong desire he did not fully understand, scarcely noticing where he was going. Out of the corner of his eye he saw a lady-in-waiting sitting on a footstool with her eyes closed and her hands folded in her lap.

He made his way down dark corridors and along passages hung with tapestries that had almost crumbled to dust. Nowhere could he see anything that could possibly be his heart's desire, and yet he gazed at everything around him with amazement and wonder.

Then he came to a door standing open. Suddenly, his heart began to beat faster, and he felt as though something was calling him from within the chamber. "I know it," he said to himself. "This is where my fate lies. There is a wonder here that I must see."

As he stepped into the room, the first thing that caught his eye was a curtained bed whose fabric was thickly covered with white lace woven from one hundred years of cobwebs. Florian drew aside the curtains and the daylight fell on the most beautiful face he had ever seen. For a moment he could not speak, and he simply stood gazing at the young woman who lay before him with her faithful dog at her feet. It was as though she had closed her eyes only a moment ago, for there was not one speck of dust on the bed, nor any sign that one hundred years had passed while she was sleeping.

"This is my heart's desire indeed!" Florian said. He leaned over her and kissed her gently, and at once her eyes opened and she smiled at him.

"I have been dreaming about you, I think," she said.

"And I have been dreaming of you," said Florian, "even though I did not know it until this moment. There is much I want to say to you."

"And I to you," Aurora answered.

They sat and smiled into each other's eyes, and the roses that had grown over the bedstead gave out a fragrance that filled the room with hope and happiness.

As the Princess awoke, so did everyone else in the palace. The King and Queen hurried to their daughter's bedroom and found there a handsome young man, dressed in clothes that looked somewhat outlandish to them.

The Queen herself took Aurora's clothes from the sandalwood chest, and upon seeing them, Florian said, "My grandmother had a dress like that when she was a young girl. As soon as you come to my castle, I will find you the most beautiful gown in the world."

A ripple of sunlight spread through the room and in the same moment the fairy of the woodland appeared at the door. The King and Queen went to greet her and to thank her for protecting their

child through the long years of her slumber.

"I see you found your way," the fairy said to Florian.

"I did," he answered. "Though it is a mystery to me how you know this."

"You were kind to me," said the fairy. "See, I still have your cloak."

"But I gave it to an old lady," said Florian.

"It suited me to hide my true form," said the fairy.

Gradually every footman, servant, and cook in the palace woke up and looked around them, amazed to see the terrible state of neglect that had overtaken all the rooms. Gardeners frowned at the state of their flower beds and groaned at the work they would have to do. In the stable, the Princess's horse woke up and snorted gently through its nostrils. Dogs began to bark and cats to meow. Where was their breakfast? Life and laughter returned to everything.

Florian and Aurora walked through the gardens, talking to each other. The sun shone down on them, and the love they felt for each other deepened as they spoke. Both were under the spell of a new enchantment as powerful as the one from which Aurora had just awoken. The Princess had many questions she wanted to ask, but there would be time enough for those later.

"Will you marry me, Aurora?" Florian asked.

"Yes," said Aurora. "I will come with you wherever you may go."

They continued walking toward the river.

Far, far away in the depths of the forest, Skura sat in her tower and felt her powers growing fainter and fainter. She stood for a moment beside the door and gathered her cloak around her. Some time later, a thin, gray cat with yellow eyes slipped out of the room, down the tower stairs, and into the darkness where it was soon lost among the trees.

The King and Queen ordered a great banquet to celebrate the marriage of their daughter to Prince Florian. The spit in the kitchen turned, and good smells of cooking filled the air. The wedding cake was decorated with garlands of sugar roses, and the Queen's ladies-in-waiting spent hours making ready the silk dress that Aurora was to wear.

After the wedding service, the feasting and dancing lasted all night, and as the dawn broke, the King and Queen kissed their daughter good-bye and wished her good luck. Then Florian and Aurora stepped into a gilded carriage, and they made their way over the drawbridge to begin a life of perfect happiness and harmony.

The End